THE GUEST

BY

JAMES MARSHALL

HOUGHTON MIFFLIN COMPANY BOSTON 1975

Also by
JAMES MARSHALL

George and Martha
George and Martha Encore
Miss Dog's Christmas Treat
The Stupids Step Out
What's the Matter with Carruthers?
Willis
Yummers!

Library of Congress Cataloging in Publication Data

Marshall, James, 1942-
  The guest.

  SUMMARY: A moose welcomes a snail as her houseguest
and his sudden disappearance causes her great concern.
  [1. Friendship—Fiction]   I. Title.
PZ7.M35672Gu   [E]   74-32043
ISBN 0-395-20277-9

          ISBN: 0-395-20277-9 Reinforced Edition
    ISBN: 0-395-31127-6 Sandpiper Paperbound Edition
          Printed in the United States of America

       G 10 9 8 7 6 5 4 3

FOR
MURIEL
KORN

One rainy afternoon while Mona was practicing her scales,
she had the oddest feeling.

"I must be catching the flu," she said to herself.

Then Mona saw the little stranger.

"Hi," he said. "My name is Maurice."

"Goodness!" exclaimed Mona. "You scared me! It's not polite creeping up on people like that."

The snail apologized.

"Would you care for some chocolate milk and cookies?" asked Mona.

When the chocolate milk and cookies were all gone, Maurice talked about himself.

"My life was getting so boring," he said, "and I decided to take a little vacation. But I've been traveling for days and days now, and I'm starting to get lonely."

Mona was all heart. "Why don't you be my guest for a few days?"

Maurice thought that was a lovely idea.

Mona was glad to have someone around the house. When she did her chores, Maurice was always there, keeping her company.

And to Mona's surprise, Maurice was an excellent cook.

"In France they actually eat little creatures like me," he said.

"I'm told we are very tasty."

Mona made a face.

When Mona was away at work, Maurice enjoyed answering
the telephone. He didn't always make it in time.

"I'm so slow," he said.

"That's OK," said Mona.

Hide-and-Seek was one of their favorite games.

On Maurice's birthday, Mona had a little party.

"I love dressing up," said Maurice.

"So do I," said Mona.

Mona couldn't have been happier.

But one day Mona noticed that Maurice was acting moody. For hours and hours he sat on the window sill and stared outside.

"Oh dear," thought Mona, "I hope I didn't say something to offend Maurice."

The next morning Maurice didn't show up for breakfast. Mona had made his very favorite breakfast too.

"Where can he be?" she asked herself. "He *loves* French toast."

She looked high and low, but Maurice was nowhere to be found.

Mona sat herself down and had a good cry.

"Maurice has left me," she sobbed.

At work Mona was all fumbles. She simply couldn't concentrate.

"You're getting sloppy, Mona," said her boss.

But Mona didn't care. All she could think about was Maurice and how much she missed him. "I hope he didn't go to France," she said with a shudder.

She decided to put up a sign, one she made herself.

But no one fitting Maurice's description had been seen.

Days and days went by.

Sometimes Mona went to the park. She looked so sad and dejected.

"Poor thing," people said. "Maybe she's lost her dog."

Mona didn't want to talk about it. She went home to practice her scales.

But as she was playing, she had the oddest feeling.

"Hi," said Maurice. "I missed the family."

Mona was so glad to see Maurice that she forgot all about scolding him for leaving without telling her.

Maurice presented Jean Pierre, Brigitte, Monique, François, Maurice Junior, Marie Louise, Jean Paul, Renée, Philippe, Georges, Claude, Suzanne, Napoléon, Louis, Marc, Antoinette, Henri, Joséphine, Jeanne, and Fifi.

"Aren't they cute?" said Mona.

Mona spent the rest of the day making French toast for all her new friends.